WANGARI MAATHAI

Get to know the woman who planted trees to bring change

by Lisa A. Crayton

a Capstone company — publishers for children

Raintree is an imprint of Capstone Global Library Limited, a company incorporated in England and Wales having its registered office at 264 Banbury Road, Oxford, OX2 7DY – Registered company number: 6695582

www.raintree.co.uk
myorders@raintree.co.uk

Text © Capstone Global Library Limited 2021
The moral rights of the proprietor have been asserted.

All rights reserved. No part of this publication may be reproduced in any form or by any means (including photocopying or storing it in any medium by electronic means and whether or not transiently or incidentally to some other use of this publication) without the written permission of the copyright owner, except in accordance with the provisions of the Copyright, Designs and Patents Act 1988 or under the terms of a licence issued by the Copyright Licensing Agency, Barnard's Inn, 86 Fetter Lane, London, EC4A 1EN (www.cla.co.uk). Applications for the copyright owner's written permission should be addressed to the publisher.

Edited by Mari Bolte
Designed by Dina Her
Original illustrations © Capstone Global Library Limited 2021
Picture research by Svetlana Zhurkin
Production by Tori Abraham
Originated by Capstone Global Library Ltd

978 1 4747 9932 4 (hardback)
978 1 4747 9934 8 (paperback)

British Library Cataloguing in Publication Data
A full catalogue record for this book is available from the British Library.

Acknowledgements
We would like to thank the following for permission to reproduce photographs: Alamy: Furlong Photography, 13, Jenny Matthews, 28; Getty Images: AFP/Gianluigi Guercia, 6, AFP/Simon Maina, 26, Corbis/Wendy Stone, 20, 24, Sygma/William Campbell, 23, ullstein bild/Claude Jacoby, 11; Library of Congress: 15; Newscom: Danita Delimont Photography/Alison Jones, 17, Polaris/Toby Selander, 5; Shutterstock: Alexandra Giese, 10, EcoPrint, 4, JonoErasmus88, 18, Joseph Sohm, cover, Pratchayanee Nualpring, 21, Sopotnicki, 8, spatuletail, 7, Toni Palm, 9. Design Elements by Shutterstock.

Source Notes
Page 4, line 5: Wangari Maathai. *Unbowed: A Memoir*. New York: Anchor Books, 2007, page 45. **Page 6**, line 18: Ibid. **Page 9**, line 7: Ibid., page 5. **Page 12**, line 10: Ibid., page 39. **Page 29**, line 22: Ibid., page 293.

Every effort has been made to contact copyright holders of material reproduced in this book. Any omissions will be rectified in subsequent printings if notice is given to the publisher.

All the internet addresses (URLs) given in this book were valid at the time of going to press. However, due to the dynamic nature of the internet, some addresses may have changed, or sites may have changed or ceased to exist since publication. While the author and publisher regret any inconvenience this may cause readers, no responsibility for any such changes can be accepted by either the author or the publisher.

Printed and bound in India

CONTENTS

Chapter 1
Future forests 4

Chapter 2
Born to lead 8

Chapter 3
Roots of change 12

Chapter 4
Tree doctor 16

Chapter 5
In full bloom 22

Glossary 30
Find out more 31
Comprehension questions ... 32
Index 32

1 FUTURE FORESTS

A fig tree stood strong and tall near Wangari Maathai's home in Kenya, Africa. In her village, people believed fig trees were **sacred**. Her mother called the nearby tree the "Tree of God". Wangari was told never to collect wood for a fire from that tree.

Fig trees provide fruit for people and animals to eat. They are also home to honeybees.

Wangari Maathai's nickname was Mama Miti, or "Mother of Trees".

A clean, gentle stream flowed near the village. As a child, Wangari often walked to it along a path lined with trees and crops such as bananas and arrowroots. One of her chores was to gather water from the stream for her family.

Throughout her adult life, Wangari spoke and wrote fondly about her childhood experiences with nature. They were key to shaping her into the woman she had become. Wangari remembered when Kenya was a country filled with wildlife, **fertile** grasslands and thick forests. She found strength in those memories when politicians and big businesses nearly destroyed her homeland in the 1960s and 1970s.

fertile filled with or capable of producing healthy plant life
sacred of high religious importance

Wangari Maathai was an environmental scientist and a women's rights **activist**. She spent her life **restoring** land and helping women. Wangari is most famous for creating a non-profit organization called the Green Belt Movement. Since 1977, the organization has encouraged people to plant more than 51 million trees in Kenya alone. Its focus is to bring communities and governments together to work for the protection of the natural world.

Wangari's love for the land ran deep. She wanted others to be able to share that love, not just during her lifetime but for generations to come. "As a child, I used to visit the point where the water bubbled up from the belly of the Earth to form a stream," she said. "I imagine that very few people have been lucky enough to see the source of a river."

Teaching people how to plant and nurture trees was Wangari's way of empowering them to make a better future.

Although Wangari faced many struggles in her work, she never gave up. She received the Nobel Peace Prize in 2004 for her efforts. She was the first African woman ever to receive the award. She died seven years later, in 2011, but her work lives on today. It still inspires people to plant trees as a way of restoring forests, land and hope for a better world.

After her death, the African country of Burundi honoured Wangari and her work with a national postage stamp.

activist a person who works for social or political change
restore to bring something back to its original condition

2 BORN TO LEAD

Wangari Maathai was born on 1 April 1940, in the village of Ihithe, Kenya. She, her five siblings, and her parents were Kikuyus, the largest **ethnic** group in the country. The group was made up of 10 smaller clans. Each clan was known for a special skill or ability. Wangari's clan was known for leadership.

Traditional Kikuyu homes were round huts with roofs of layered, dried grasses.

Wangari was born during the rainy season. For months, large amounts of rain fell and soaked the land. The local people welcomed it. Rivers and streams filled with clean drinking water. Many types of crops such as wheat, beans and corn grew well. So did fruit and nut trees. "As long as the rains fell, people had more than enough food for themselves, plentiful livestock and peace," Wangari later wrote.

As a tenant farmer, Wangari's father didn't own the land he farmed. He rented it. He grew crops and sold them to the landowner, a British man. Wangari's father made very little money. Yet he loved his job and the land. He passed on that love to his children.

Wangari's mother worked in the fields, planting and harvesting crops. She took her daughters, including Wangari, with her.

Corn makes up a large part of the Kenyan diet.

ethnic relating to a group of people sharing the same national origins, language or culture

Elephants can be dangerous when protecting their young.

Thanks to her parents, Wangari developed a deep, long-lasting respect for nature at an early age. She learned about wildlife and how to spot animals that could be dangerous. Elephants, leopards and other animals lived in the forest near her home. She was careful but not afraid. Her mother taught her to be brave.

Wangari was a curious child. She enjoyed learning and explored as much of the outdoors as she could. She didn't go to school, though – at least not at first. Her family believed in education but they held to their culture's traditional ways. Traditionally, boys went to school, while girls stayed at home to help their families with chores. Wangari's father had gone to school as a child and could read and write. Her mother did not go to school and was unable to do either.

Wangari's two older brothers went to school in Nyeri, Kenya. At the age of seven, Wangari moved to Nyeri with her mother to be closer to them. The move would change her life.

Traditional ways

When Wangari was a child in Kenya, women were not considered equal to men. Boys went to school. Girls did not. Men were the leaders of their families. They could usually choose the jobs they wanted. Most women stayed at home. They cooked, cleaned, sewed and cared for the children with their daughters' help.

3 ROOTS OF CHANGE

In Nyeri, Wangari helped her mother with household chores during the day while her brothers were in school. She also helped with crop planting and harvesting, fetching water and cooking. When the boys returned home each day, Wangari asked them lots of questions about what they'd learned. One day, her 13-year-old brother asked their mother why Wangari didn't go to school. Their mother paused for a moment, then said, "There's no reason why not."

Wangari started school soon after that. She loved it and got good grades. In 1959, Wangari proudly graduated from high school. She did not know what kind of job she wanted after leaving. There were few options for young Kenyan women at that time. She could be a nurse or a teacher. Wangari did not want to be either.

The village of Nyeri, Kenya, in the early 1960s

What Wangari really wanted was to go to university. That was a big goal, especially when most local girls didn't finish high school. But Wangari got lucky. She heard about a new programme that had been created for Africans to attend university in the United States. Wangari applied and was accepted. She was even given a **scholarship**. With hope and a willingness to work hard, she headed to the United States.

To study abroad

The "airlift" programme was a partnership between a handful of Kenyan and American leaders to send young African men and women to study in US universities. About 800 students travelled to the United States as part of the programme between 1959 and 1963. The idea was that, once educated, the students would return home to better their countries by sharing their knowledge, skills and experiences.

scholarship an award to help pay for schooling

Wangari attended Mount Saint Scholastica, in the state of Kansas. Because of the deep connection to the living world she'd made back in Kenya, she studied **biology**. She graduated in 1964 with a bachelor's degree. She then continued her studies in biology at the University of Pittsburgh, Pennsylvania, graduating in 1966 with a master's degree.

Being in the United States changed Wangari. As a black woman especially, she felt transformed by the many things she learned outside of the classroom. The 1960s were a time of great unrest in the country. Black people faced intense struggles. They fought to gain equal rights, to be treated the same as white people. Their fight eventually inspired women across the country to stand up for the same rights as men. In areas such as pay and job opportunities, the gap between women and men was large. Wangari firmly believed that all people should be treated equally, regardless of race or gender.

The US Civil Rights Movement

The Civil Rights Movement in the United States lasted from 1954 to 1968. During that time, African Americans held **protests** to demand equal treatment as white people. Violence broke out between white and black people across the country. In the end, things did change for the better. New laws were passed, including the Civil Rights Act of 1964. The act ended **segregation** throughout the United States and made it illegal to deny people their basic rights based on race, colour, religion, sex or the country they came from.

DID YOU KNOW?

Wangari met Mwangi Mathai in 1966 and married him three years later. They had three children together. After the couple divorced in 1979, Wangari added an extra "a" to her last name. It was a way for her to signal a fresh start in her life, without changing her name completely.

biology the study of plant and animal life
protest the act of speaking out about something strongly and publicly
segregation the practice of keeping groups of people apart, especially based on race

4 TREE DOCTOR

Wangari returned to Kenya after finishing her master's degree. She studied at the School of Veterinary Medicine at the University of Nairobi, the capital city. When she graduated with a PhD in 1971, she made history. She was the first woman ever to earn such a degree in Central or East Africa. The university immediately offered Wangari a teaching job, which she accepted.

While Wangari had been in the United States, Kenya had gained its independence from Great Britain. It was now a free country. But the Kenyan people still held on to some British ways. For example, they followed the practice of cutting down trees and forests to make room for tea, coffee and other **cash crops**. This practice is called **deforestation**. It was destroying Kenya. The loss of trees and forests affected the land, water and animals. Sadly, Wangari saw the rich, green land of her childhood quickly disappearing.

Deforested land can quickly turn desert-like, harming local plants, animals and people.

A free country

Native Africans have lived in what is now Kenya since c.2000 BC. Through the years, other peoples arrived, including peoples from the Arab Peninsula, Iran and Portugal. They established **colonies** during various periods in history. Control of the land changed with each new colonial power. Kenya became an official colony of Great Britain in 1920. It went on to gain its independence in 1963.

cash crop a plant grown to sell, rather than to be used by the grower
colony a territory settled by people from another country and controlled by that country
deforestation the act of removing large areas of trees

Wangari knew that the roles trees and forests play in an environment are many. They help regulate local climates and weather. A number of animals live and raise their young in forests. They find shelter in trees from harsh weather. Many animals eat the trees' fruit, nuts and leaves. People also use trees for some of the same reasons.

Giraffes live in parts of Africa. They feed mostly on leaves, especially those of acacia trees. Giraffes may eat up to 34 kilograms (75 pounds) of food per day.

Trees also help to protect the environment. Their roots filter underground water to keep streams and rivers clean. They grip the soil and stop it from washing away. In these and other ways, trees help keep forests, communities and countries healthy. Without them, land, water, wildlife and people suffer.

Deforestation in Kenya also cut down on the amount of available firewood. People used wood from trees as a fuel to cook their food and heat their homes. Fewer trees meant less firewood. Without firewood, families found it hard to cook well-balanced, nutritious meals. Many people started eating processed foods that needed less cooking. Poor diets led to declining health.

Wangari soon heard about troubles Kenyan women were having. Women in **rural** areas said they had to walk great distances to find clean water for their families. They said they didn't have enough firewood to cook meals.

rural of the countryside; away from cities and towns

As Wangari listened, she realized that the big issue causing the women's problems was **environmental degradation**.

But what could the women do to start restoring the land? How could they heal the environment? Wangari thought she might have the answer. Her suggestion to the women was to plant trees.

It was an obvious solution, but at the time, there were no local community programmes in place for bringing back the forests. Wangari invited other women to partner with her in planting trees. She first asked women in rural areas. They were willing and able to help, but they needed some training and encouragement. That's when the idea for the Green Belt Movement was born.

Wangari set out to save her country one small sapling at a time.

DID YOU KNOW?

Some crops and trees can't exist well together. The Green Belt Movement teaches farmers the importance of growing native species – plants that are well-adapted to the local environment. Farmers are urged to plant crops and trees that grew well together in Africa before cash crops became popular.

Soil erosion

Trees provide shade for people, animals and soil. When trees are cut down, soil is no longer held in place by tree roots. It also has no protection from **erosion**. Steady rain and hard winds can cause the soil to wear down or wash away. Sun can scorch soil, drying it up. When soil is destroyed, crops can't grow. Farmers lose their harvests. People go hungry or even starve. Others get ill or die from poor diets. Planting trees helps to enrich the soil. It reverses the bad effects of erosion.

environmental degradation a severe decline in the health of the natural world

erosion the wearing away of soil by water or wind

5 IN FULL BLOOM

On 5 June 1977, hundreds of people followed a marching band through the streets of Nairobi. They walked to a popular park on the edge of the city. Everyone had gathered for a tree-planting ceremony for World Environment Day.

Seven trees were planted that day. They honoured seven former community leaders of Kenya, men and women, who had lived in the 19th and early 20th centuries. Wangari was at the park too, shovel in hand. The tree-planting ceremony had been her idea. The National Council of Women of Kenya, of which Wangari was a member, organized the celebration. It was part of the council's new tree-planting programme called "Save the Land Harambee".

DID YOU KNOW?

Harambee means "Let us all pull together" in Swahili, an African language. It encourages unity and teamwork.

Wangari's sunny personality and background in biology made her an excellent "tree teacher".

The tree-planting also marked the official start of what would become the Green Belt Movement. Wangari created the programme to bring change to Kenya by restoring forests. Its name came from the way the green trees were planted – in a row, or belt.

Wangari believed the Green Belt Movement could solve a number of problems. Firstly, it would restore Kenya's land and make it more suitable for growing food. Secondly, it would provide cleaner water. And thirdly, it would help women earn money and learn new skills, empowering them in their communities. Educating people about how to care for the environment and themselves was key.

Women from Kenya's rural areas eagerly gathered to learn about the Green Belt Movement's mission.

Planting a tree is so easy, anyone can do it!

That's the message Wangari shared with women about tree-planting over the next few decades. People called her Mama Miti. The nickname means "Mother of Trees" in the Swahili language. The Green Belt Movement provided interested women with seedlings and taught them how to nurture the seedlings until they were tall enough to plant in the soil. Women were paid a small amount of money for every tree that grew.

At first, government leaders helped Wangari with her mission. But then they stopped. They started seeing her as a threat to their power. Some didn't like seeing a woman be so successful and outspoken. They didn't like her teaching poor people how to take ownership of their lives. Also, it was believed that only educated foresters should plant trees.

In 1999, armed guards tried to block Wangari from planting trees in a forest near Nairobi, Kenya.

Wangari worked hard to try to protect the environment. She also fought for human rights and **democracy** throughout Kenya. Her efforts often put her in danger, and her life was threatened many times. She was attacked and beaten. She was arrested and thrown in jail. But even so, Wangari did not give up. She focused on bringing hope to her country – one tree at a time.

Wangari tried every way she could to bring positive change to Kenya. She even ran for president in 1997, at the age of 57. She lost that election, but she was elected to **parliament** in 2002. She won with an incredible 98 per cent of the vote. She soon became the assistant minister of environment, natural resources and wildlife. This government position allowed Wangari to help protect her homeland in official, long-lasting ways.

DID YOU KNOW?

The Green Belt Movement's work is funded in many ways. Government grants provide money. So do foundations and environmental groups. Gifts of trees or money come from businesses and individuals around the world.

democracy a form of government in which the people elect their leaders
parliament a group of people who have been elected to make laws

Wangari received the Nobel Peace Prize in 2004 for her environmental work and her efforts to advance democracy and peace. She was the first environmentalist and first African woman to win the prize.

Wangari wrote about her life in a book called *Unbowed: A Memoir*, first published in 2006.

28

In 2009, Wangari was named a Messenger of Peace for the United Nations. Both this award and the Nobel Peace Prize allowed her to travel the world. She spoke tirelessly about protecting forests. She shared the importance of forests and trees in relation to climate change. And she encouraged people everywhere to do what they could for the environment. A few years later, in 2011, Wangari died from cancer at the age of 71.

Today, the Green Belt Movement continues the work Wangari started. It has shared its ways of working with organizations and communities in more than 30 countries. People have teamed up to provide Earth-saving programmes. In 2006, Wangari inspired and helped lead the Billion Tree campaign, which had a goal of planting 1 billion trees around the world. It met its goal by late 2007, and there's now a *Trillion* Tree campaign in place.

Wangari was often asked how to help make a difference. Her answer was usually the same: plant a tree. "After all," she wrote, "trees are living symbols of peace and hope."

GLOSSARY

activist a person who works for social or political change

biology the study of plant and animal life

cash crop a plant grown to sell, rather than to be used by the grower

colony a territory settled by people from another country and controlled by that country

deforestation the act of removing large areas of trees

democracy a form of government in which the people elect their leaders

environmental degradation a severe decline in the health of the natural world

erosion the wearing away of soil by water or wind

ethnic relating to a group of people sharing the same national origins, language or culture

fertile filled with or capable of producing healthy plant life

parliament a group of people who have been elected to make laws

protest the act of speaking out about something strongly and publicly

restore to bring something back to its original condition

rural of the countryside; away from cities and towns

sacred of high religious importance

scholarship an award to help pay for schooling

segregation the practice of keeping groups of people apart, especially based on race

FIND OUT MORE

Dr Wangari Maathai Plants a Forest (Rebel Girls Chapter Books), Eugenia Rebel Girls (Rebel Girls, 2020)

Environmental Activist Wangari Maathai. (STEM Trailblazer Bios), Jennifer Swanson (Lerner Classroom, 2018)

Little Dreamers: Visionary Women Around the World, Vashti Harrison (Puffin, 2018)

Wangari Maathai: The Woman Who Planted Millions of Trees, Franck Prévot (Charlesbridge Publishing, 2017)

What Would She Do?: Real-life Stories of 25 Rebel Women Who Changed the World (Carlton Books Ltd, 2019)

WEBSITES

Wangari Maathai
www.greenbeltmovement.org/wangari-maathai

Wangari Maathai Foundation
www.wangarimaathai.org

Woodland Trust: How trees fight climate change
www.woodlandtrust.org.uk/trees-woods-and-wildlife/british-trees/how-trees-fight-climate-change/

COMPREHENSION QUESTIONS

1. How does deforestation harm the environment? Explain its effects on the land, people and animals.

2. In traditional Kenyan society, women had little or no access to the education that men had. Leadership and economic power belonged to men. In what ways did Wangari inspire and empower women?

3. Planting one tree at a time to fight environmental degradation is an example of small acts solving large problems. Think about your own life. How would doing a number of small things make a large difference to yourself or others?

INDEX

"airlift" programme 13
attacks 26

Billion Tree campaign 29
birth 8, 9

cash crops 16, 21
childhood 4–5, 6, 8–13, 16
children 15

death 7, 29
deforestation 16, 19

education, Wangari's 12–14, 16
erosion 21

father 8, 9, 10

government roles 27
Great Britain 9, 16, 17
Green Belt Movement 6, 20, 21, 23–25, 27, 29

Kenya's independence 16, 17
Kikuyus 8

marriage/divorce 15
Mathai, Mwangi (husband) 15
mother 4, 8, 9, 10, 11, 12
Mount Saint Scholastica 14

National Council of Women of Kenya 22
Nobel Peace Prize 7, 28, 29

siblings 8, 9, 11, 12

traditions, Kenyan 10, 11
tree benefits 18–19, 21
tree planting 6, 7, 20, 21, 22–25, 29
Trillion Tree campaign 29

United Nations 29
United States 13–14, 15
university 13–14, 16
University of Nairobi 16

University of Pittsburgh 14
U.S. Civil Rights Movement 14, 15

women's rights 6, 14
World Environment Day 1977 22